+ SAFETY FIRST

Staying Safe
# On the School Bus

**by Joanne Mattern**

**Reading consultant:** Susan Nations, M.Ed.,
author/literacy coach/consultant in literacy development

**Please visit our web site at: www.garethstevens.com**
**For a free color catalog describing Weekly Reader® Early Learning Library's list**
**of high-quality books, call 1-877-445-5824 (USA) or 1-800-387-3178 (Canada).**
**Weekly Reader® Early Learning Library's fax: (414) 336-0164.**

**Library of Congress Cataloging-in-Publication Data**

Mattern, Joanne, 1963-
    Staying safe on the school bus / by Joanne Mattern.
        p. cm. — (Safety first)
    Includes bibliographical references and index.
    ISBN-13: 978-0-8368-7795-3 (lib. bdg.)
    ISBN-13: 978-0-8368-7802-8 (softcover)
    1. School children—Transportation—Safety measures—Juvenile
literature.    2. School buses—Safety measures—Juvenile literature.
3. Safety education—Juvenile literature.    I. Title.
    LB2864.M3519    2007
    363.12'59—dc22                                2006030337

This edition first published in 2007 by
**Weekly Reader® Early Learning Library**
A Member of the WRC Media Family of Companies
330 West Olive Street, Suite 100
Milwaukee, WI 53212 USA

Managing editor: Valerie J. Weber
Editor: Barbara Kiely Miller
Art direction: Tammy West
Cover design and page layout: Charlie Dahl
Picture research: Diane Laska-Swanke
Photographer: Jack Long

The publisher thanks Sage and Judi Austin, Josie, Daniel Burss, Tyler Cartagena, Christopher Ginter, Michael
Hanke, Christina Kingsawan, Amber and Tayler Kozelek, Maria Najera, Rubie Rowe, Temple Woods,
Lukas and Maria Zabel, Garrett Bennett, Tammy Janichek, Patty Raschig, and Riteway Bus Service for their
assistance with this book.

Printed in the United States of America

1 2 3 4 5 6 7 8 9 10 10 09 08 07 06

## Note to Educators and Parents

Reading is such an exciting adventure for young children! They are beginning to integrate their oral language skills with written language. To encourage children along the path to early literacy, books must be colorful, engaging, and interesting; they should invite the young reader to explore both the print and the pictures.

The *Safety First* series is designed to help young readers review basic safety rules, learn new vocabulary, and strengthen their reading comprehension. In simple, easy-to-read language, each book teaches children to stay safe in an everyday situation such as at home, at school, or in the outside world.

Each book is specially designed to support the young reader in the reading process. The familiar topics are appealing to young children and invite them to read — and reread — again and again. The full-color photographs and enhanced text further support the student during the reading process.

In addition to serving as wonderful picture books in schools, libraries, homes, and other places where children learn to love reading, these books are specifically intended to be read within an instructional guided reading group. This small group setting allows beginning readers to work with a fluent adult model as they make meaning from the text. After children develop fluency with the text and content, the book can be read independently. Children and adults alike will find these books supportive, engaging, and fun!

— Susan Nations, M.Ed., author, literacy coach,
and consultant in literacy development

Here comes the school bus!
Let's learn to ride safely.

Wait for the bus on the **sidewalk** or grass.

sidewalk

7

Make sure the bus stops before you go near it.  Hold on to the **handrail**.  Walk slowly up the steps.

handrail

9

Pick a seat and stay seated.

11

Keep your head and hands inside the bus.

Help the bus **driver** keep you safe.  Do not shout or throw things in the bus.

FIRE EXTINGUISHER INSIDE

MAX. CAP. 71

Time to get off! Make sure your stuff does not get caught on the bus.

Walk away from the bus carefully.  The driver must be able to see you go.

Wait for cars to stop before you cross the street. Have a safe bus trip every day!

# Glossary

**alarm** — a sound, light, or other signal that warns people about danger

**bullies** — people who are mean to other people or who try to hurt them

**fire drill** — the practice of the right way to get out of a building in case of a fire

**practice** — to repeat something many times so you can get better at it

**recess** — a short time to rest or play during the day

# For More Information

## Books

*Hello, School Bus!* Marjorie Blain Parker (Cartwheel)

*Molly Rides the School Bus.* Julie Brillhart (Albert Whitman and Company)

*My School Bus: A Book About School Bus Safety.* My World (series). Heather L. Feldman (PowerKids Press)

*Safety on the School Bus.* Safety First (series). Lucia Raatma (Bridgestone Books)

## Web Sites

NHTSA's Safety City Bus Safety
*www.nhtsa.dot.gov/kids/bussafety/index.html*
Click on the bus to learn lots of ways to stay safe.

School Bus Safety Web
*www.ncbussafety.org/NCBUSSAFETY.html*
Safety tips and games teach how to stay safe riding the school bus.

# Index

# About the Author

Joanne Mattern has written more than 150 books for children.  She has written about weird animals, sports, world cities, dinosaurs, and many other subjects.  Joanne also works in her local library.  She lives in New York State with her husband, three daughters, and assorted pets.  She enjoys animals, music, going to baseball games, reading, and visiting schools to talk about her books.